To my sisters, Sarah and Katie, with GINORMOUS apologies for all the times I played 'Earthquakes' with your dolls' houses – D.M.

For Doug the Dog, fearless chaser of his own tail – R.M.

Kelpies is an imprint of Floris Books
First published in 2022 by Floris Books

Text © 2022 David MacPhail. Illustrations © 2022 Floris Books
David MacPhail and Richard Morgan have asserted their rights
under the Copyright, Designs and Patent Act 1988 to be identified
as the Author and Illustrator of this Work

Also available as an eBook

British Library CIP Data available
ISBN 978-178250-785-7
Printed & bound by MBM Print SCS Ltd, Glasgow

Floris Books supports sustainable forest management
by printing this book on materials made from wood that
comes from responsible sources and reclaimed material

MIX
Paper from
responsible sources
FSC® C117931
FSC
www.fsc.org

VELDA THE AWESOMEST VIKING

and the GINORMOUS Frost Giants

Written by **David MacPhail**

Illustrated by **Richard Morgan**

Young Kelpies

MEET THE CREW of
THE MANGY MUTT

NISSA

**VELDA
THE
AWESOMEST
VIKING**

HENNA

MANDRAKE

BRIDIE

LORD EGBERT

SISTER AKUBA

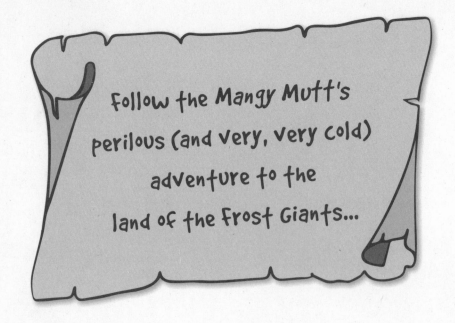

Follow the Mangy Mutt's
perilous (and very, very cold)
adventure to the
land of the frost Giants...

Chapter 1

The Vikings were a funny lot.

They believed the Earth was flat. They believed that if you died with a sword in your hand you'd be carried off to Viking heaven, known as Valhalla. And that if you stuffed a small radish up your nose far enough you could tickle your brain and good ideas would fall out.

They also believed that it was bad luck – *boat-sinkingly* bad luck – to have girls on board their longships. So bad that deadly krakens would rise up out of the sea and drag them down to their watery DOOM!

Yes, that bad.

So, you can imagine the horror when a whole boatload of female Vikings – with only a couple of males thrown in – sailed into the Danish trading port of Elsinore.

As the longship approached the pier, some men on the harbourside pointed out the ship's ragged sail with disgust. Most Viking sails bore an image of a wolf or a dragon, or a man playing keepy-uppy with his enemy's head. But – SHOCK HORROR! – this one had a multi-coloured patch that looked rather like a rainbow. A RAINBOW, INDEED! Rainbows were about the least Vikingy thing in the world since the invention of cutlery.

"Terrible!" spat one old red-faced man, resting on his stick and grinding his gums.

"An outrage!" agreed a second, shaking his fist as the new arrivals disembarked. "They'll bring a curse down on us!"

PEEE-OOOOOOOO-EEE!

A loud noise rudely interrupted their complaining. It sounded like someone slowly deflating a balloon. For a second, they almost thought it sounded like a...

They turned to see an ancient woman with crinkly brown skin and greying dark hair. She was grinning, wearing furs and carrying a long, curved bow. She was also accompanied by a horrible cabbagey stench.

"Ex-CUSE me!" one of the men croaked. "Did you just...?"

"Fart? Yes," replied the woman. "Now which way is the castle?"

The old men pointed up the hill. "My thanks," she replied, before thumping the two of them on the head with her bow. They crumpled to the ground, unconscious.

A short while later, in the castle's keep high above the harbour, Elsinore's ruler, Count Stollenberg, was happily humming as he counted his money.

He paused briefly to admire his smooth, pale reflection in the mounds of shiny silver coins, then ran a hand through his glossy hair.

Suddenly, there was an almighty **CRASH!**

Stollenberg lost count, which annoyed him, but also secretly gave him a lovely warm feeling inside, because he'd have to start again, and ohhh, how he loved to count his money! Wasn't it marvellous to be a handsome count who counted handsomely?!

He turned to see that his door had been smashed to smithereens. A tiny girl strode into the room. Curly red hair poked out from under an oversized helmet. Her rosy, wind-chapped face broke into a smile, and she twirled a massive axe.

"Wotcha!" she said brightly. "Count Snottyberk, I presume?"

Chapter 2

"The name's *Stollenberg*, actually!"
The count summoned his
most forbidding (and yet
still *extremely* handsome)
expression. "Who are you?
And where are my guards?"

Velda nodded over her
shoulder. "They're having a little nap."
Stollenberg glimpsed a pile of unconscious bodies
outside the door. He felt his nostrils flare, which, as he
checked his reflection, actually made him look even
MORE attractive. Still, he wasn't happy. He'd spent a

fortune on those guards and their fancy uniforms, and the idiots had been bested by this child!

There were two women standing with Velda. The first was tall and athletic, with warm brown skin, and was wearing a nun's habit. This was Sister Akuba. The second was the fur-wearing farter from the harbour, whose name was Henna of Greenland. They were all part of the same Viking crew.

"What do you want?" Count Stollenberg demanded. "I'm a *very* busy man."

Velda tested her axe blade with her finger. "My friend here, Sister Akuba, heard something very interesting on the nun network."

Stollenberg frowned. "The nun network?"

"We nuns communicate with each other, you know," said Sister Akuba. "Even the ones sworn to silence, who have to do charades."

Velda continued. "Seems you swindled some local nuns out of their convent."

"Oh, that!" Stollenberg replied, feeling his cold heart brighten, for he'd SO enjoyed throwing the nuns out onto the street. Although 'swindled' was a bit unfair. After all, the nuns did break their contract. One of their rent payments was a whole *twelve hours* late. It wasn't his fault that a storm had blocked the road, and the donkey carrying the money got sick, and the ferryman carrying the donkey across the river died of the plague... blah blah blah! "Excuses, excuses! They should have read the small print."

"We also heard you're now using the nuns' convent to store your collection of handcrafted jewelled underpants," added Sister Akuba disapprovingly.

Stollenberg shrugged. "A man needs to keep his

underwear somewhere. And mine is so expensive! I can't just stuff them in a drawer. Anyway…"

He looked Velda up and down. "What do you care about nuns? You're just a little girl!"

"SAY THAT AGAIN! I DARE YA!" Velda snarled, and she leapt at Stollenberg, swinging her axe. Sister Akuba grabbed Velda and held her back.

"She doesn't like being called 'just a little girl', and we don't like seeing people getting ripped off,

so you'd better give the convent back," Sister Akuba suggested, struggling to restrain Velda.

"Or what?" sneered Stollenberg. He was *very* good at sneering. He put it down to his icy blue eyes. But this angry little hooligan and her friends weren't scared.

Velda scowled. "Or… we're going to take what you took from the nuns back from your vault. Plus interest!"

"Oh, are you now?" Stollenberg rose to his feet. He was very tall, and he found this was a good way of bullying people (and also of getting a good view at royal banquets, which was a bonus). "And how do you plan on doing that?"

"Oh, easy." Velda nodded at the cast-iron door of Stollenberg's personal vault. "I'm just going to stroll in there and take it."

He laughed. "I'd like to see you try." One hand twitched towards his sword, which was encrusted with tiny sparkly diamonds. Almost as sparkly as his perfect white teeth. The other hand went to protect his special top-secret key, which was dangling from his—

His fingers clutched at the air near his belt hook, and he looked down to see...

A seagull. Quite a large one, with murderous eyes. And his special key was grasped in its sharp yellow beak.

Count Stollenberg *hated* seagulls. One had once pooped on his most expensive hat and the stain had never come out. "Give that back this instant!" shrieked the count, but the seagull waddled away and dropped the key in Henna's outstretched palm, who then passed it to a grinning Velda.

"Thanks!" she said sweetly.

Count Stollenberg leapt to get the key back, but he was thwarted by the gull. It flapped its wings and pecked the jewels on his cloak, hoping they were food.

"Begone, foul beast!" Stollenberg cried, waving his arms about, but he was powerless as the winged

fiend chased him around his counting table, while Velda, Henna and Sister Akuba unlocked his vault.

"See?" said Velda. "Told you I'd just walk right in!"

"N-N-NOOOO!" the count spluttered. "Not my lovely money!"

Stollenberg now knew how normal people felt when their goldfish died, or their pet dog got run over. He'd ditched his own relatives long ago, so the contents of his vault were the closest thing he had to a family.

In a last, desperate attempt, he reached for the rope that pulled the alarm bell, which would bring guards rushing to his side, but Henna **THWACKED** him on the head with her bow.

"Night night," she grinned. "Do not let the seagulls bite!"

Chapter 3

"YAAA!" Velda flicked the horse's reins as she steered the wagon full of Count Stollenberg's dosh downhill through Elsinore's winding streets. Henna and her scary-eyed gull sat tight beside her, while above, Sister Akuba glided down from the castle on a rope. Handily, before becoming a nun she'd had many jobs, including a circus acrobat.

Behind, Stollenberg's men followed on their fearsome warhorses. Fearsome, but slow. The guards' ridiculous uniforms weren't much use in a chase: their pointy helmets crowned with colourful feathers

got tangled in the washing lines that criss-crossed the street. The horsemen slashed at the laundry with their swords, but kept getting a face full of underpants. To delay them even further, Henna scattered some of the stolen money behind the wagon, and the watching townspeople swarmed to pick up the coins, blocking the way.

At the harbourside, Velda brought the wagon skidding to a halt beside her ship, the *Mangy Mutt*, with a **SCREECH!** "Right, you snivelling dogs," she barked at her waiting crew, "let's load this dosh up and get going!"

"Och, leave it to me, Boss," said a young girl with red hair tied in a messy ponytail and freckled fair skin. She wore a tartan shawl over a grubby apron. This was Bridie of Forfar, the ship's cook.

"NOOO, not you!" cried Velda, because while

Bridie made excellent butter biscuits, she was also a bit of a butter*fingers*. But it was too late; she had already heaved one of the sacks over her shoulder, not noticing that it was the wrong way up and all the silver was spewing out.

"Is it just me or is this sack getting lighter?" Bridie asked cheerfully, while the others leapt to sweep up the trail of coins behind her.

One of only two men in Velda's crew was Mandrake, a pale, tufty-haired Irish bard. He suddenly gave a cough, which was never a good sign as it usually meant he was about to sing. His instrument of choice – or rather, his weapon of torture – was his harp, which he now strummed.

TW-OINNNGGG!

Then he burst into song, sounding like a walrus with tonsillitis:

"Load up the gold, oh stash it in the hold,
It makes me itch, we're stinking rich!
Oh quick, load up the gold."

Normally this would be Velda's cue to throw
something heavy at Mandrake to shut him up, but
she needed him to sing so that Nissa, her navigator,
could steer the boat. Nissa was an excellent sailor,
but after her head was nibbled by a polar bear she
had forgotten how. For some unknown reason, noise
was the only thing that brought back her memory.

She was currently standing idly nearby, mewing
at a harbour cat, her helmet perched on top of her
heavily bandaged head. On hearing the music, she
jumped to the longship's steering tiller. "Oh, thanks
Mandrake... All set, Velda!"

With the loot finally aboard, they were ready...

Well, almost, for there was still one crew member ashore.

Lord Egbert (who was a real lord, though you'd never know it) was a withered old Anglo-Saxon gentleman with a bushy white moustache. He'd come aboard Velda's ship mistakenly thinking it was a luxury cruise and never left. During their recent shore visits he'd taken to entertaining children with magic tricks he'd learned during the crew's long journeys at sea. He'd taken to it SO much, in fact, that he now dressed like a magician, including long black cloak, top hat and bow tie. He was surrounded by a gaggle of local children on the side of the harbour.

"And for my next trick," he cried, "prepare to be **AMAZED!**"

A good magician might expect gasps of wonder when they performed, but Lord Egbert usually drew

gasps of horror instead. It was hardly surprising.
Velda had seen rabbits pulled from inside hats
before, but never a hat pulled from inside a rabbit.
The rabbit wasn't the only one turning green.

"TA-DAAAH! Now, how about another *hare*-
raising trick?" Lord Egbert asked with a chuckle.

Velda latched a grappling hook onto Lord Egbert's
collar and yanked him aboard the ship. "Soz, but it's
time for the vanishing act!"

They pushed the longship away from the pier, just as Stollenberg's guards charged out of the crowd. Their ridiculous helmets were festooned with holey socks and faded knickers.

"Get rowing, you slovenly pig-dogs!" Velda bellowed to her crew. They manned the oars and the ship quickly moved towards the harbour entrance.

Things were looking **UP**, but then suddenly they were looking **DOWN**, for a huge horn sounded from the castle battlements high above them.

A-WOOOOOO!

Soldiers on the harbour wall began to wind a creaking wheel, and a set of giant metal gates appeared from inside the stone walls. They CLAMPED shut over the harbour entrance like a dragon's teeth around prey.

Bows were drawn and spears raised, all aimed towards Velda and her crew.

Velda's fingers twitched excitedly on the handle of her axe. Excellent – a fight! "Come on! We can take 'em!" she cried.

But then a gigantic crossbow manned by two soldiers on the harbour wall aimed a flaming arrow right at the belly of the *Mangy Mutt*. The words *SHIP SINKER* were carved on the crossbow's side, along with dozens of notches. A third soldier stood beside it, gleefully readying a piece of chalk to record another victim.

Sister Akuba placed a gentle hand on Velda's arm. "Not this time, Velda."

Velda eyed the flaming arrow, and then with a frustrated "GRRRR!" she reluctantly let go of her axe.

Chapter 4

Count Stollenberg rubbed the bump on his head as he watched the guards march the prisoners up through the town. The tiny red-haired girl strode out in front, threatening the men escorting her to the point of tears, and occasionally stopping to wave at the gawping crowd.

Stollenberg was angry, and not just because the townspeople were cheering. He'd punish them for that later. Perhaps he'd cancel Yule, or place a tax on birthday presents, so that any time someone bought someone else a gift, they'd also be buying one for him... Hmm, that was a lovely thought, but one for another day.

Mostly he was angry because his fortress had
been breached. Hadn't Elsinore been voted Europe's
strongest castle four years in a row in *Siege Magazine*?
He glanced at the magazine parchments he'd framed
and hung on the wall of his keep. If it got out that
a team of girly Vikings had waltzed right into his
personal vault, his reputation would be in tatters.

But worst of all was that he'd been *tricked*. He was *always* the trickster, *never* the trickee! Luckily, he'd managed to catch them before they got away, but STILL… That girl and her friends had hoodwinked him.

The Captain of the Guard interrupted him with a cough. "My Lord, are you sure we should have these prisoners inside the castle?" He cast a furtive glance around and whispered, "You know, the *curse*. Everyone says girl Vikings bring bad luck."

"Oh, don't worry, they won't be here long."

"What do you mean?" asked the Captain.

"I've just had a devilish idea," said Stollenberg, with an extremely devilish but extremely handsome grin.

Velda and her crew were chained up, back-to-back,

in the middle of a huge chamber full of all sorts of treasure.

There were paintings and statues, not to mention some odd items shut away in glass cases – a golden fleece, an ornate jewelled lamp, and a shining sword bearing the word 'EXCALIBUR' on its blade. There was also a strange white thorn bush in the corner of the room. It seemed to glow faintly.

"ATTENNN-SHUN!" barked a voice, and in marched two of Stollenberg's biggest, toughest guards. Unfortunately, the effect was ruined when they got jammed together in the doorway thanks to their fancy puffed-up uniforms. Velda and her crew erupted in laughter.

While the guards struggled, Velda whispered to the others, "Quick, while those two clowns are busy, can anyone get free?"

"I have a chisel up my sleeve that might help," murmured Sister Akuba. Blacksmithing had been another of her jobs before she became a nun. "But I can't reach it."

"Ach, here, let me," replied Bridie, and she wiggled her arms behind her back.

Sister Akuba giggled. "Stop, you're tickling!"

The two guards were still straining to free themselves. "Hurry up!" hissed Velda.

"Sorry," said Bridie, before she whipped out the shiny chisel. "A-haaa!"

"YES!" said Velda, but this soon turned into "NOOOO!" when the tool slipped out of Bridie's hand, clattering on the stone floor and landing where nobody could reach it.

"Anyone got any other tricks up their sleeve?" asked Velda.

"*The Great Egberto* at your service!" announced Lord Egbert, who was still wearing his top hat, though it was looking a bit worse for wear. He made a big show of struggling with his hands, before whipping out a bunch of fake flowers. *"TA-DAAAH!"*

Velda rolled her eyes. "Very helpful – NOT!"

"AAARGH!" The two stuck guards suddenly lurched forward and fell to the floor with a *CRASH!* They had been shoved out of the way by Count Stollenberg, who now stood in the doorway, grinning like a very wicked (but very dashing) wolf.

Chapter 5

Count Stollenberg stepped over his guards and slithered into the room. "Sorry about all this." He waved his hand at the mounds of jewels and shiny objects. "I don't really do dungeons. They're so ugly. And where's the profit in locking people up? You have to feed them, and pay for jailers. Then there's the insurance, the healthcare, inspectors." He admired himself in the reflection from one of the many glass cases. "Oh, it's a nightmare."

"Let me out of these chains, Lord Smug-Face, and I'll show you a nightmare!" growled Velda. She was eyeing the exits. There was one window, right next to the big white thorn bush in the corner. But the sheer rock face outside meant it would be a steep drop.

Stollenberg ignored Velda, though his eyes flicked to Henna's seagull to make sure it was in chains too. It was, and was currently trying to eat its way out of them without much success.

Satisfied, Stollenberg continued. "This is my treasure room, where I keep all of my legendary riches. I'm a bit of a collector. There are one hundred and thirty-three other rooms in this castle, including my own personal vault, which you tried to steal from, and FAILED." He grinned.

"You're just a big show-off, aren't you?" said
Velda.

Stollenberg leaned into her face, giving a small
laugh. "And you, what are you, *little girl*?"

Velda snarled a vicious snarl and snapped her
teeth. The count jumped back. Now it was Velda
who grinned. "I'm a VIKING!"

"A pretty awesome one too," Bridie chipped in.

"We sail the seas, going on adventures and raining down violent vengeance on slimy slimeballs like you!" Velda explained.

Stollenberg's brow furrowed. "Hmm, sounds *exhausting* to me."

"It's better than sitting in a stupid castle all alone counting money!" Velda replied.

Perhaps she had a point, thought Stollenberg. If only he had someone to share his riches with… But then, his own family had never been remotely interested in money or fine things. Brutes! His pondering was interrupted by Mandrake, who was whimpering. He didn't deal well with being held prisoner. "And who are you?"

Mandrake attempted a bow, only to crack his chin on the chains. "I-I am N-Nandrake, Bing of Cards."

"He says he's Mandrake, King of Bards," explained Bridie. "He gets his words mixed up. That's why he sings."

"Oh, I could use a good-quality bard around here," said Stollenberg.

This brought a gale of laughter from Velda and her crew. Mandrake's face flushed with anger. "Nat is FOT THUNNY!"

"He says it's not funny," translated Bridie, suppressing a giggle.

Stollenberg rolled his eyes, reminding himself he needed this ridiculous crew for his plan...

"You know," he said, with a dazzling fake smile, "I'm not outwitted very often, but your raid took me rather by surprise today. I was impressed."

"You ain't seen nothin' yet, Count Floppy-Hair,"

said Velda, straining against her chains. "Just wait till I'm free!"

"Hmm, I don't suppose…" he said, "that in exchange for that freedom, you'd be interested in a deal?"

Velda stopped straining and eyed him suspiciously. "What *kind* of a deal?"

Chapter 6

Count Stollenberg wiped a smudge off the glass case holding the gold-coloured fleece. "You see that I'm a collector of precious things, but there's one item I've been after for years. I *reeeaaalllly* want it, and I want you to steal it for me. You're clearly talented… and rather terrifying."

"Steal for *you*? No chance!" scoffed Velda.

"As well as your freedom, I will give you a reward," he said. "A BIG one."

Velda was curious, despite herself. "What is this item you want me to steal?"

"The legendary Frost Hammer. It once belonged

to the mighty Norse god Thor, but now the *disgusting* Frost Giants have it."

Velda watched the veins bulge in the count's temples. "I *really* hate those Frost Giants! Filthy, ugly brutes. They don't deserve to own such a thing!"

Bridie gasped. "Frost Giants?!"

The count strode over to the white thorn bush in the corner of the room. Velda wondered what was precious about it. "I'll give you two sacks of silver for the nuns," he went on, an oily smile replacing his anger. "They can buy another convent with it. Plus, two for yourselves. Fair's fair. What do you say?"

In the silence, Henna gave a small, whiney fart.

PPRRRRFFFTTT!

Velda nodded. "OK, Duke Dirtbag, you've got a deal."

"Velda!" Sister Akuba cried.

Mandrake burst into tears. "NOOO! I'm poo falented to die!"

But Velda just grinned.

Like always, she had a plan.

Most Vikings called their ships tough-sounding names, like *Spear-Belcher*. Velda's ship was called the *Mangy Mutt*. It was the name it had come with, and she hadn't liked it at first but it was growing on her, mainly because it annoyed people. Velda *really* liked annoying people.

As Velda and her crew boarded the *Mangy Mutt*, Stollenberg stepped out from amongst the guards who had escorted them to the harbour. "Oh, I almost forgot…" he said. "I'm keeping your bard as a hostage. Can't have you skipping off on me, can I?"

Velda scowled. **RATS!** She'd been planning to do exactly that! She looked around for Mandrake, only to see him boxed in behind some spearmen. His head bobbed over their shoulders as he jumped up and down, whimpering, "Oh, but my bends feed me!"

"He says his friends need him," translated Bridie.

"What use is a bard on a mission like this?" said Stollenberg. "He'd be useless."

"Yes. But he's *our* useless bard. Give him back!" Velda snarled.

"Of course," said Stollenberg. "As soon as you return with the Frost Hammer." He turned to

Mandrake. "On the bright side, you can sing for me here. I'm a lover of good music."

Velda and her crew tried very hard to contain their sniggering, but eventually they failed, collapsing in hysterics. *"HAHAHAHAHA!"*

Stollenberg frowned. "Anyway, you'll find the Frost Hammer far to the north at the Hall of the Frost Giants in Jotunheim. A map and clothes for the cold weather are aboard your ship. Can't have you getting lost and dying of frostbite, can we?" He smiled, looking as if he would like nothing more. "Bring me back the Frost Hammer and you'll have your bard, *and* your silver." With a dramatic swish of his cape, he strutted down the dock like a model on a catwalk.

"He has SO practised that in the mirror," grumbled Velda.

Mandrake gave a solemn cough. "Wery vell. Then I snall send you off with a snog."

Velda gagged. "EURGH, NO THANKS!"

"A song! He's going to give us a *song*," translated Bridie.

"EURGH, NO THANKS!" said Velda again, but Mandrake strummed his harp anyway.

TW-OINNNGGG!

"Farewell, farewell,
I hope the wind doth quell
Your cries of woe
To see me go..."

Velda jabbed some lobster pots piled on the dock with her axe, and the whole stack crashed down, burying Mandrake beneath. Only his blond quiff poked out the top like a tuft of long grass.

"We'll be back for you soon, Mandrake!" called Velda. "Maybe."

Mandrake's hand shot up between the lobster pots and gave a sad wave as the *Mangy Mutt* pushed off, gliding through the harbour gates and out into the open sea.

Chapter 7

"What do we do now, Velda?" asked Bridie.

Velda stared round at her crew. She should have known that snake Stollenberg would pull a trick like that! Now they couldn't just leg it like she'd planned, not if she wanted Mandrake back. The bard might mix his words up and sing like a hyena with a headache, but he was one of her crew, and that meant something.

"Let's sneak back in and break Mandrake out," suggested Sister Akuba.

The others murmured their agreement, and Velda cast a vengeful eye back at Elsinore fading into the horizon. Oh, how she'd love to do that! But as much as she wanted to catapult Stollenberg into the sea, the man wasn't stupid. They'd taken him by surprise the first time. Doing it a second time wouldn't be so easy. He'd be ready for them.

Velda's temper snapped. She whipped out her axe, raised it high above her head, and brought it smashing down onto an empty crate with a yell, splitting it into pieces. **THWACK!**

"No," she said, feeling better already. "But don't worry, I've got a plan B!" She stepped up on an old barrel and the crew gathered round. "We ARE going to steal the Frost Hammer!"

The crew gabbled excitedly, except for Henna and her seagull, who, for some reason known only to her, kept screaming "PEANUTS! PEANUTS!" over everyone.

"We're really going up against the Frost Giants?" asked Sister Akuba warily.

"Aye, they're GINORMOUS!" said Bridie.

"SO?!" said Velda, propping her fists firmly on her hips. "Say what you like about Count Toffee-Nose, but he was right about one thing: we *are* terrifying! And we're clever and resourceful, and if there's a Viking crew who can pull this impossible heist off, it's us!"

"OORAH, Boss!" they all cheered.

Velda barked an order at Nissa. "Now, take us east!"

"Oh, er…" Nissa scratched her chin and looked confused.

"Ack!" sighed Velda. "Mandrake's not here!" Nissa relied on the bard's 'singing' to make her memory come back. "Does anyone know any songs?"

The only songs Velda knew were Viking belching songs. She tried one out, but it just made everyone want to belch, including Nissa, which sent her steering askew and nearly tossed them all overboard.

Next Henna tried out some seal-singing, but all that did was – surprise, surprise – attract lots of seals.

"The one thing about Mandrake's singing," shouted Velda over the honking sound of the excited seals, "is that it didn't attract *anyone*."

"Enemy ships steered clear," agreed Sister Akuba.

"I once saw him drive off a shark with just a strum of his harp," added Lord Egbert, and they all nodded fondly. "Magical!"

Bridie, they found, couldn't hold any sort of tune, as she belted out a song about a man from her homeland called Donald who had lost his 'troosers'. This set the crew arguing about where this Donald character might have mislaid his trousers, and why.

Velda was about to get out the pots and pans and start bashing when Sister Akuba saved the day, singing a rather rude sea shanty (for a nun, anyway).

"That's it!" cried Nissa, gripping the steering tiller. "My memory is coming back!"

"Then let's get going!" yelled Velda, hoping Sister Akuba knew more than one rude song about bottom-burping Vikings.

Chapter 8

As darkness fell, the *Mangy Mutt* passed through the perilous Skagerrak Straits, then turned north, skirting the coast. The water was icy, the wind was cold and snow topped the steep, rocky cliffs. Everyone bundled on the fur coats Count Stollenberg had provided and huddled around the ship's brazier.

"So, how *do* we steal the Frost Hammer?" asked Sister Akuba, who'd taken a break from singing. "I mean, we're not *actually* going to fight these Frost Giants, are we?"

The nun had a good point. Velda would have a go at anyone, but taking on Frost Giants might be a bit much, even for her. She watched Lord Egbert practising a magic trick with a mouse he'd found in the ship's food stores, then Henna's seagull cast its hungry glare in the mouse's direction. The creature took fright, running up Lord Egbert's sleeve.

"EEEK!" The old man danced about as the mouse ran all over his body. That gave Velda an idea.

"They're giants, right? So to them, we're tiny. Like mice." The others nodded.

"So… we'll be like mice, sneaking in underneath their feet, and back out again. They won't even notice us!"

"In the stories, giants have a keen sense of smell," said Bridie. "What if they sniff us out?"

"PAH! That's just in stories," said Velda.

"What do you know of Frost Giants, Bridie?" asked Sister Akuba. "It might be helpful."

"Just what I've read," the cook replied. "My old master, he let me read his books; it stopped me breaking things."

"He sounds like a goodly man," said Sister Akuba.

"Aye, until one night I tripped over his baffies, dropped a candle and set fire to his library…"

"Baffies?" asked Velda.

"Ach, his slippers," explained Bridie. "Anyway, the Frost Giants' Hall is deep inside a huge mountain. The king of the Frost Giants lives there and he's called Thrum. He has a daughter called Princess Gerda and a son called Olaf, who mysteriously disappeared years ago."

"How does something as enormous as a giant disappear?" scoffed Velda.

Bridie shrugged. "The stories didn't say."

Velda thought about this while watching Lord

Egbert dance around trying to catch the mouse. "Oh, er, hee hee," he giggled, "excuse me, friends, but might I have your ass-heeee-heeee-assistance?"

Bridie rushed over to try and rescue him from the mouse (or perhaps the other way round, as the creature had taken a wrong turn and got lost in the old man's underpants).

There was still something nagging at Velda. Something about Stollenberg. "I don't get it. Why does the count hate the Frost Giants so much, and

why is he so desperate to have this Frost Hammer? He already has a room full of shiny junk. It has to be more important than he's letting on."

"You saw all his treasures," said Sister Akuba. "To him, things matter more than people. I feel sorry for him."

"Hmm," said Velda. "Now he's got Mandrake singing for him all day, I almost feel sorry for him too!"

They carried on through the icy, white-capped sea for days until they came to the Bay of Serpents, marked on Stollenberg's map. Velda didn't see any snakes, which was REALLY disappointing, cos by now she was itching for a scrap.

Before long, they came close to the shore, and Henna pointed towards a village nestled in the snow not far off. "That village is called Berken. From here the map says we must travel onwards by foot," she said.

As the *Mangy Mutt* crunched onto the snow-crusted sand, Velda heard panicked screams and shouting coming from the village. That raised her spirits!

"Trouble!" she cried. "Brilliant, let's go!"

Chapter 9

The village square was in chaos. People were
SCREAMING! and SHOUTING! and RUNNING!
Velda burst into the square, yelling like a banshee.

"Where's the battle?" she cried.

An ancient-looking man with a stooped back and a long beard stopped to stare. He was loading some even more ancient people (if that was possible) into a wagon. "Haven't you heard?" he whined, as Velda's shipmates arrived behind her.

"Spit it out, Grandad!" said Velda.

"The FROST GIANTS!" he croaked.

Velda's ears pricked up. "What about 'em?"

"They're having a wedding, you fool!"

Velda was about to knock the old man over the bonce for calling her a fool, but Bridie interrupted. "If they're having a wedding, that might be important."

"Important?! Dangerous more like!" answered the old man.

"Dangerous?" asked Velda, getting excited.

"Like turning-up-by-accident-in-the-middle-of-a-polar-bear's-birthday-party kind of dangerous!" said the man.

"Brilliant!" said Velda brightly.

"I once got stuck on a drifting iceberg with a polar bear," announced Henna as she calmly stroked her gull's head.

"What was that like?" asked Nissa.

"Disappointing. There was no party."

"King Thrum's daughter, Princess Gerda, is

getting married," explained the man as he struggled to mount his wagon. "So the Frost Giants are looking for humans to be her bridesmaids."

"Why does she want human bridesmaids?" asked Velda.

"Oh, I remember reading about this," said Bridie. "Legend has it that the princess thinks humans are *really* cute."

"That's right," wheezed the old man. "She plays with humans like *you'd* play with a little doll."

Velda twirled her axe. Now she was *definitely* going to whack him. "The only time I've been near a doll is when I've used it for target practice, Grandad!"

Sister Akuba placed a hand on Velda's arm. "Peace, little one, we need this man's information."

Meanwhile, Lord Egbert had taken the opportunity to entertain the panicking villagers with

magic tricks. He'd found an abandoned wooden
chest and had set it up in the middle of the square.
He was grinning and wielding a rusty old saw.
"Would anyone kindly volunteer to be sawn in
half?" Cue more SCREAMING! and SHOUTING!
and RUNNING!

"How far is Jotunheim from here?" Velda asked.

"You wish to go to the land of the Frost Giants?!"
The man gave a hoarse laugh, which soon turned
into a coughing fit. Velda had to leap up and slap
his back a few times before he could speak again. "If
you're mad enough," he eventually wheezed, "it is a
day or so's march, that way." He pointed north.

Velda eyed an old sledge and a herd of mangy
reindeer scratching their bums on a fence post.
"We're going to need transport." She turned back to
the man, who was limply trying to flick his horse's
reins, but failing miserably. "Oi, Grandad, can we
borrow that sledge?"

"Feel free," he replied. "We're heading south
where there is no snow, and no Frost Giants!"

"Excellent!" Velda slapped one of the man's
horses on the rear. It whinnied and sped off, pulling

the old man with it so fast his false teeth flew out. Henna's gull instantly swooped down and picked them up, hoping they might be food, but the gnashers got wedged in the bird's open beak. The terrifying sight was enough to scare off the remaining villagers.

As the last wagon joined the escape, Lord Egbert, still wielding his rusty saw, shrugged sadly. "They were a tough audience."

Chapter 10

Velda and Sister Akuba picked out the least grumpy
and flea-ridden reindeers from what was a very
grumpy and flea-ridden herd, and attached them to
the sledge.

Nissa came running back from the ship. "I've
left one of our 'long,
painful death' notes."
This was a note promising
a long, painful death to
any trespassers who tried
to steal the *Mangy Mutt*
while the crew were away.

If you are readin'
this note you are
in for a LONG,
PAINFUL DEATH!

Signed,
the crew of
the Mangy Mutt

The notes were Velda's idea. She'd wanted to give them out to everyone they met, but Sister Akuba had persuaded her against it.

"Alright, let's get going, you verminous clods!" barked Velda, and they all crammed into the sleigh. With a crack of the reins they were off.

"Are we nearly there yet?" grunted Henna after barely a minute had passed. "My small friend gets cranky when he is hungry."

"We've only gone a hundred yards!" snapped Velda. "And he's always hungry!"

"Perhaps a magic trick would help!" declared Lord Egbert. He wrenched his arms free from between their squashed-together bodies and began shuffling a deck of cards. "Now, which card am I holding up?" He whisked his hand in the air, but unfortunately most of the cards came with it, having frozen to his fingers.

"Looks like all of them," said Sister Akuba.

"Oh, well, *freeze* things happen!" He spent the next hour flapping his hands around, trying to unstick the cards. This at least provided the others with some entertainment, which was more than could be said for his actual magic tricks.

They glided across the snow, the reindeers carrying them over snowy hills and valleys, with only an occasional stop to scratch at their fleas. After crossing wastes of ice and snow they reached a forest of tall pine trees.

"Let's rest here for the night," said Velda. They halted and huddled around a campfire. It was so cold everyone's teeth were chattering, even the gull's false ones.

"Bad news, I'm afraid. My last bannocks have frozen solid," said Bridie, bashing two of her oaty cakes together with a loud **CLUNK!**

"So we have nothing to eat?" said Sister Akuba.

"I could defrost them for you," offered Henna. "But I would have to sit on them."

"No thanks!" said Velda with a sigh.

"Anyone got any jokes?" asked Nissa brightly.

"I hear no human who ventured inside the Frost Giants' Hall ever made it back out alive," said Henna.

Nissa burst out laughing and slapped her thigh, then stared round at all the gloomy faces. Her laugh died out. "Er, I might have forgotten what a joke is."

"Where did you hear this?" Velda asked Henna.

Henna nodded at her gull. "My friend told me. He hears things from the other birds." The gull made a **SCREAMING** sound. "He would also like me to say that he is very disappointed by the lack of peanuts on this trip." The bird gave them all a death stare.

"So what if no one has made it out alive!" snapped Velda. "We'll have to be the first." Without the Frost Hammer she could not rescue Mandrake or get the nuns' silver back. Besides, she was beginning to fancy a crack at fighting a real Frost Giant.

Sister Akuba looked like she was building up to saying something she knew Velda was NOT going to like. "That man said the Frost Giants are seeking out bridesmaids. Why don't we—"

"Can I just stop you there!" interrupted Velda. "Cos I know where this is going, and the answer is NO! There's no way I'm being a bridesmaid. Itchy dresses and flower-holding and smiling... NO THANKS!"

"But it might be the easiest way into King Thrum's Hall—"

"I don't care," growled Velda. "I'm not doing it. Not now, not EVER! We'll just have to find another way in."

Chapter 11

Velda and the crew woke to find Nissa staring at
something on the ground just behind their camp.
"Er… excuse me, everyone, but why does this big
dip in the snow look like a massive footprint?"

Velda went
over to look.
"Because it *is*
a footprint. A
giant's footprint!"

They gathered
round the huge
dent in the snow,

which they could only see now thanks to daylight.

"We must be getting closer," said Velda. "Come on, let's get going!"

They travelled all morning through howling blizzards, until they caught sight of a humungous ice-covered mountain through a break in the trees.

"There it is!" barked Henna, checking the map (the bits her gull hadn't eaten, anyway). "The Frost Giants' Mountain."

"And that's the way in." Sister Akuba pointed out a huge door set into the rock.

"The only way in, I'd bet," added Velda. "And the only way out."

"Ach, don't be so sure." Bridie nodded to a dark spot higher up on the mountain. As Velda looked closer she could see that it was some sort of chimney. Yet there was no sign of any smoke.

"What is it?"

"A belch stack, most likely," grunted Henna.

"A what?"

"Giants belch a lot."

"Even more than us Vikings?" asked Velda, impressed.

Henna shrugged. "They are ten times bigger,

at least. That is a lot of belch. The chimney would carry it off."

"Well, I'm not going in that way." Velda grimaced. She was as hard-belching as any good Viking, but abseiling through a dense cloud of stinky giants' gas was a bit much, even for her. "It's the front door for us. Come on!"

Chapter 12

The doorstep to the Frost Giants' mountain home was so high Sister Akuba had to give everyone a leg up. The door was taller than the tallest pine, and wider than the longest longship. Velda gazed up at it and gave a whistle. "Right, you lot! Look out for any gaps we can squeeze through. We're mice, remember!"

"Shh! Someone's coming!" hissed Sister Akuba.

Only now did Velda hear the **THUMP! THUMP! THUMP!** of a giant stomping in their direction. The crew leapt from the doorstep into a mound of snow, watching as a line of giants began to appear from the nearby woods.

"They must be here for the wedding," whispered Bridie.

There were all different sorts of giants. Some were dressed in animal skins and leafy crowns (Forest Giants). Others wore leather aprons and skull caps (Fire Giants, who forged weapons for other giants deep inside volcanoes). There were even Sea Giants, carrying huge tridents and garbed in seaweed cloaks. One by one, the enormous creatures trooped up to the door and gave a knock with a mighty **BOOM! BOOM! BOOM!**

"WHO GOES THERESIE?" came a thunderous voice from within, and a spyhole in the door slid open to reveal a massive googly eye.

Each time a giant gave their name, the googly eye would stare at them for a second. "GOOD NEWSIE-WOOSE! YOUR NAMESIE IS ON THE LIST."

The door would swing open and the giant would trudge inside, then the door would slam shut again.

As Velda watched, she spied a large boulder next to the doorway. "If we hide behind there, we can sneak in after the next giant," she whispered. "Easy!"

So they all shuffled over to the boulder, as small and as silent as mice, and waited. Soon – **THUMP! THUMP! THUMP!** – they heard another giant approach.

The giant gave the door a bash, and the googly eye appeared. "Get ready to leg it inside, everyone," whispered Velda.

There was an ominous pause. Velda looked up, and UP, and UP to see a female Forest Giant. She was sticking her nose in the air and taking a huge sniff. "I SMELLZ SOMETHIN!" she boomed in a deep voice.

"Oh, are we playing guess the smell?" said Nissa. "I love this game, although the answer is usually Henna."

"SHHHH!" hissed Velda. "Everybody stay perfectly still!"

There was an ear-splitting CRREEAAKK! as the front door opened. It turned out that the very large googly eye was attached to a very large giant: a Frost Giant, with a snowy beard and blueish skin. He leaned out and took a sniff too. Velda watched his brow furrow, making a noise like cracking ice, before he answered. "NOSIES, I DO NOT SMELLZ ANYTHIN! NOW COMESIE IN."

The two giants went inside and the door slammed shut with a **BANG!**

Velda seethed. "Grrr! How do we get past this door?!"

"WEH-EH-ELL," said Sister Akuba hesitantly. "We could just knock and volunteer as bridesmaids."

Velda roared and sunk her axe into the snow. "For the last time – I. AM. NOT. BEING. A. BRIDESMAID!"

"Ach, maybe we should just use that belch stack thing," suggested Bridie. "It cannae be any worse than the stench of Henna's farty bahookie."

Velda groaned. It was hardly the stuff of Viking legend – floating in on a cushion of whiffy gas – but it was at least slightly better than having to wear an itchy dress. "FINE!" she grumbled. "The belch stack it is."

They climbed the snowy mountainside, and were nearly frozen solid by the time they reached the belch stack. Squinting through the icicles attached to her eyelashes, Velda peered down into the darkness, wafting away stinky fumes with her hand. "UGH! It smells like an elk's bottom down there."

Henna took a large sniff. "No, I have smelled worse."

"You've smelled something worse than that?!" Velda asked, amazed.

"I mean *I* have smelled worse," replied Henna with a proud smile.

Velda sighed. "Come on, let's get this over with."

She secured her grappling hook, threw down her rope and began to lower herself into the dark. The others followed.

Unfortunately, the rope only went so far and it soon ran out. If they wanted to get inside the Frost Giants' Hall, if they wanted to retrieve the Frost Hammer and rescue Mandrake, there was no other option…

"Alright, after me, everyone," cried Velda. "3, 2, 1…
JUUMMP!"

Chapter 13

"WAAAAAGGHHHHHHHHH!"

There was darkness, and falling... a LOT of falling. Velda braced herself for a hard landing, but instead felt something soft and bouncy.

BOINNNGGG!

"WHEEE! Is this some kind of foul-smelling funfair?" asked Nissa, bouncing past her.

The crew bobbed **UP**, and **DOWN,** again and again, until they landed in a pile. Henna's gull, who had flown down, landed easily on top of them all, then tried to eat Lord Egbert's top hat.

"AAAIIIIEEEE!" A GINORMOUS

ear-splitting squeal rattled Velda's eardrums, and she looked up to see a huge pair of ice-blue eyes staring down at them.

A Frost Giant! This one was female, with bluish skin and hair that hung down in great snowy sheaves from her massive head. She was wearing the fluffiest, sparkliest wedding dress any of them had ever seen. Velda and her crew had landed in her lap.

The giant gave a snort and clapped her hands in excitement.

"WHAT A LOVELY SURPRISIE! HOOMAN BRIDESMAIDSIES!"

Velda sagged. "You'll be Princess Gerda."

"And we, it seems, will be bridesmaids after all," added Sister Akuba.

Velda felt like hitting something. Very hard. "Oh, great!"

An older male Frost Giant stood nearby. He had a long icy beard and a frosted crown perched on top of his head.

"That must be her father, King Thrum," said Bridie.

"OH!" said the king with surprise as he spotted the crew. "I THOUGHT WE HAD NOT FOUND ANY BRIDESMAIDSIES, BUT I SEE YOU FOUND

THEMSIES ALL BY YOURSELFY-WELF, MY
LIKKLE POPSICLE."

"WHY, YEEES!"
squealed the princess,
giving Velda earache.
"THEY JUST FELLED
INTO MY LAPSIE-
WAPSIE. AND THEYS ARE
PERFECTY-WERFECTY,
DADDY-WADDY!"

King Thrum
smiled, displaying
huge gravestone-
sized teeth. "WELL,
HURRY YOURSELFY!
YOUR GUESTIES ARE
WAITING!"

95

"WON'T BE A MOMENTSY-WOMENTSY, DADDY-WADDY!" The princess scooped up Velda and her crew in a massive hand, whisking them to a dressing table. She plonked them in front of an enormous mirror.

"NOW, TEENY-TINY HOOMANS! MEE-SIES IS GOING TO GIVE YOU-SIES A MAKEOVER!"

Chapter 14

"WHAT DID SHE SAY?!" asked Velda, a look of horror on her face.

"She's going to give us a makeover," said Bridie.

"Oh no she's not!" Velda growled, rolling up her sleeves, but for once, there was nothing she could do to stop it.

With a flick of her finger, Gerda flipped open a box as big as a house, crammed with GIMUNGOUS bits of make-up.

First, she grabbed a furry powder puff, which was about the same size as a grizzly bear. Velda wondered if it might once have actually *been* a grizzly bear. The princess snatched each one of the crew in turn and began shoving the puff in their faces.

Velda struggled, but the giant's fingers were too strong. Wafting away clouds of sparkly blue dust, she stared down at herself and roared. "AARGH! Is this… GLITTER?!"

"Och – ACHOO!" sneezed Bridie.

"I once fell into a pit of fish guts. It was not as bad as this," spluttered Henna. Her gull spluttered too, then on discovering it couldn't eat the powder puff, tried to start a fight with it instead.

"Remember!" coughed Sister Akuba. "This is our way into King Thrum's Hall, so just get it over with!"

Princess Gerda was singing as she worked. "TRA-LAA-LAAAA!" She was clearly enjoying herself. Next, she delved into her box and plucked out a tube the size of a milk churn, which was full of a kind of sparkly lipstick. She snatched up Lord Egbert, who raised his top hat. "Good day to you, madam! Would you like to see a magic tri—" She cut him short by smearing the lipstick across his face.

Finally, the giant princess yanked baby-blue
bridesmaid dresses over their heads. They all looked
like glittery blue meringues.

"NOOOO!" Velda roared, trying to crawl away.
"Kill me now!"

No detail was spared, as the princess plonked
flowery headdresses on their heads and popped tiny
bouquets of flowers into their hands.

"GORGEOUSIE-WORGESIE, MY LIKKLE HOOMANS! NOW YOU ARE READIES FOR MY WEDDEN!"

Velda glared at herself in the mirror. "NO! I WON'T DO IT!" She went to throw away her bouquet, but Sister Akuba stopped her.

"Velda, we're so close!" said the nun. "Think of Mandrake."

Velda growled. She reached for her axe, which Princess Gerda had also given a makeover. "I'd rather fight my way in! It's got to be better than this!"

"Ach, but why fight, Boss?" said Bridie. "When the princess is going to carry us." She nodded at the huge tray of ice the giant was carefully placing the crew onto one by one.

DOOOOONNNNGGG! A thunderous gong sounded from the depths of the mountain.

"OH DEARSIES, I MUSS NOT BE LATE FOR MY OWNSESS WEDDEN!" The princess whisked the tray into the air. "COME ON, LIKKLE HOOMANS. IT'S TIMESIES!"

Chapter 15

Princess Gerda carried Velda and the others down a long passageway lit by blue-flamed torches. The ceiling was covered in veins of thick frost, and portraits were etched into the icy walls. Most of them seemed to be of the same giant: a young male who looked a bit like Princess Gerda. He had her piercing blue eyes and snowy white hair. Something about the giant felt oddly familiar to Velda.

"That's Prince Olaf," whispered Bridie, reminding Velda of the story of King Thrum's missing son. Velda tried to peer closer to get a better look, but they had arrived at a vast doorway.

"The Great Hall!" said Bridie.

"How do you know?" asked Sister Akuba.

"It's written up there." She pointed out some strange lettering above the door.

"You can read that?"

"Yes, it's *Jotunn*, the old giant language. I read about it before I, och, y'know, burned my master's library down."

The Frost Giants' Hall was truly GIGANTIC. Immense stalactites hung down from the ceiling, and a table as tall as a regular castle's walls stretched along the centre. Gerda bellowed, "IT'S ME-SIES!" and the giants sitting around it turned to face her.

"AH! IT'S YOU-SIES!" King Thrum got to his feet, prompting all the other giants to push their chairs out and stand. A sleepy-looking giant stood at the king's side, slumped into a huge horn. The king nudged him with his elbow, jolting him awake, and the horn player began to puff out a tune. It was supposed to be a wedding march, but it sounded more like a moose with its head caught in a fence.

Velda clutched her ears. "That's AWFUL!"

Bridie clasped her hands to her chest. "Awww, it reminds me of Mandrake."

Princess Gerda dropped the ice tray on the tabletop with a thump. "TA-DAAAAAAH!" Velda and her crew spilled out among the plates.

"OOH, YOU GOTSES SOME BRIDESYMAIDS AFTER ALL!" came a voice, as the giants all peered closer.

"ARE THEY NOT SOOOOOO CUTESY-WOOTSEY?" Gerda beamed.

"I have not been called cutesy-wootsey before," said Henna, with her flower garland askew. Her seagull, also clad in a small dress, was NOT impressed.

A Fire Giant grinned and waggled his huge sausagey fingers at Gerda. "COO-EEE!" Velda took him to be the groom.

Gerda gave a squeal of delight, sounding like a yodelling sea lion. She ran round the table – **_BOOM!_** **_BOOM! BOOM!_** – and leapt into the groom's arms with enough force to demolish a small town.

King Thrum clapped his hands. "FIRSTIES, WE SHALL HAVE OUR FEASTIE, AND THEN THE WEDDEN!"

"Doesn't the feast usually come after the wedding?" asked Sister Akuba.

"Aye," said Bridie, "but giants dinnae do anything without eating first. In the stories they've a fearsome appetite."

There was a **GONG!**, and a parade of Frost Giant servants trooped in carrying platters piled high with food: huge steaks, mounds of roast goat, boiled hams and stewed elk, which must have just been tiny snacks for the enormous giants.

"Oh, I am SO hungry!" said Velda, eyeing the food enviously.

"I can't remember the last time I ate," added Nissa. "Actually, I *really* can't…"

Far from stopping them, the giants encouraged them to tuck in. "EATS UP, LIKKLE HOOMANS!" boomed the king.

Velda shrugged. She couldn't steal a legendary artefact on an empty stomach, could she? She and her crew launched themselves at the food. They tore it apart with their teeth. Grease smeared their make-up and gravy ran down the front of their dresses. Velda did her best to rub it in a bit more.

"MY OH MY, I HAVE NEVER SEENSES SUCH HUNGRY MAIDENSES!" said King Thrum.

"You know," said Velda, spraying food everywhere as she talked with her mouth full, "you lot really aren't so bad."

"Quite nice, actually," agreed Nissa, accepting a massive chunk of meat from a giant's fingers.

"You wonder why everyone's so scared of them," added Sister Akuba, wiping her mouth.

The giants were all laughing and singing and eating and belching. While they were busy, Velda's eyes wandered, looking for any sign of the legendary Frost Hammer. It wasn't easy, for the giants were banging the table as they sang, which caused her to bounce UP and DOWN along with the empty plates. Lord Egbert was fully enjoying himself, breaking out into some kind of dance. It was either that, thought Velda, or he had food poisoning.

Velda noticed King Thrum had stopped singing, and looked rather sad. As he sunk his chin into his hand, she spotted something behind him, something that glowed. It wasn't the Frost Hammer. Still, it was something she recognised: a white thorn bush.

"Scuse me, your Kingness," she called up at him. "But what's that?"

"OH, HELLO, LIKKLE HOOMAN," he replied. "THAT IS US GIANTSES' SPELL TREE. ITS CAN PERFORMS POWERFUL MAGIC! THERE USED TO BE TWO, BUT ONE WAS STOLENS." The king sighed. "DISAPPEARED, JUST LIKE MY SON, OLAF. OH, I MISSES MY BOY!"

Stolen, eh? thought Velda. And she knew exactly who by. Count Stollenberg had obviously paid some other crew to pilfer the precious object for him. But she still didn't understand why he hated the Frost

Giants so much when they seemed so nice, or why he wanted all their stuff.

Now that Velda had King Thrum's attention, she thought of asking about the Frost Hammer. But she didn't have to. Suddenly the king belched the most enormous belch – *"BUUURRRRP!"* – and rose to his feet. "BRING IN THE FROST HAMMER!" he roared. "ITS IS TIMESIES FOR THE WEDDEN!"

Chapter 16

"WHEEE! IT'S WEDDEN TIME!" howled Princess Gerda.

A barefooted servant entered the Frost Giants' Hall carrying a VAST velvet pillow. King Thrum plucked something tiny from it and thrust it into the air. It had a solid wooden handle topped by a thick block of gnarled blue ice. It didn't look like much in King Thrum's gigantic fingertips, but the giants roared in celebration.

"Is that it?!" Velda said through the din. She wasn't impressed, thinking that it would be bigger, but she was also quite relieved. At least it would be easier to steal.

"The Frost Hammer can break any spell. And, whoever wields it has complete power over all the giants," said Sister Akuba.

"*Complete* power? How do you know that?" asked Velda.

"That lady giant over there told me." Sister Akuba nodded her head towards a female Sea Giant who was stuffing a whole herd of roasted elk in her mouth. "Giants are very talkative when they are eating." The nun grimaced, wiping flecks of giant drool from her tunic.

"NOWSIE, WE CAN BEGIN!" declared King
Thrum, placing the hammer back on its cushion.

During the wedding ceremony, Velda tried to sneak
towards the hammer, but every time she did, huge
fingers swept her back towards the middle of the table.

When the ceremony ended, Princess Gerda
screeched with joy, then swooped her new husband
up in her arms.
The Fire Giant
gave a whimper
as she landed a
GINORMOUS
smooch on his
cheek, like a
kraken devouring
a longship.

"MMMMWWWAH!"

King Thrum waved at his servant, and Velda watched in horror as the Frost Hammer was whisked away.

"Wait! Where is he taking it?" she called up at the king.

King Thrum tapped the side of his nose with his finger. "IT IS A SECRETY-WECRETY!"

RATS! No wonder, Velda thought, *if whoever wields the hammer can control the giants…*

"We need to get after it!" she hissed to her crew.

"Quick, this way!" Sister Akuba led them towards the table corner, but they were thwarted when giant hands shepherded them back to the tray Gerda had carried them in on.

"NOWSIES! TIME FOR DESSERT!" King Thrum stood up, then levelled a finger at Velda and her crew. "LOVELY, TASTY ***HOOMANS!***"

Chapter 17

"Er… Did he just say 'dessert'?!" asked Velda, looking round at all the HUMUNGOUS hungry eyes and licking lips.

"Well, now we know why nobody wanted to be a bridesmaid," said Bridie.

"And why everyone in the village was running away," added Sister Akuba.

Lord Egbert raised his hat. "Good giants, I am not a pudding!"

"He *is* you know, a bit of a pudding," said Velda to Nissa.

"Ooh, are we having pudding?" asked Nissa.

So much for the giants being nice! Velda sized up their escape options, which were looking pretty bleak.

Bleak, but not impossible. Nothing was impossible, not while she had her trusty axe and crew at any rate.

"I've had enough of this!" Velda tore off her flowery headwear and bridesmaid's dress (she might have jumped up and down on them a bit too). The others followed her lead.

While she twirled her axe, Henna drew her bow, Nissa raised her sword, and Bridie whipped out her iron griddle pan and readied one of her frozen bannocks to use as a missile. They were ready for a fight, though the giants didn't pay any heed as they pushed their forks towards them.

"STOPS WRIGGLING, LIKKLE PUDDENS!" said Princess Gerda.

"We need a diversion! Anyone?" Velda bellowed.
Lord Egbert bowed, then stepped forward with
a swish of his cape. "I am **The Great Egberto**, master of
magic!"

"OOOOH, ENTERTAINSMENT!" gasped the giants, putting down their forks.

Lord Egbert held up a golden coin. "You are about to see something vanish in front of your very eyes."

He danced around with his hands in the air, passing the coin between his fingers. The giants watched, enrapt. Unfortunately, when he came to the great reveal, the coin hadn't vanished at all! What's more, he was baring his knobbly knees for all to see, his trousers having fallen down around his ankles during all his prancing about.

Velda groaned and sunk her head into her hands, but the giants surprised her by bursting into applause.

"WHAT A FANTABULOUS TRICKSIE!" declared King Thrum. "MORE, LIKKLE MAGIC HOOMAN!"

"Now I shall perform an even greater vanishing
act!" Yanking up his trousers, Lord Egbert strode across

to a crack in the table. Only now did Velda realise that the giants' table was not one table, but two pushed together, and Lord Egbert was standing over the join.

He whisked a blanket-sized napkin in the air, winking at Velda and the others. Velda instantly guessed his plan.

"Lie down, everyone!" she hissed.

The crew lay down on either side of the crack, while Lord Egbert flung the napkin over them. "I will make these humans… disappear!"

The enthralled giants gave an "OOOH!"

After a wave of his hands, he whipped the napkin away to reveal… an empty tabletop. *"TA-DAAAH!"*

"OH MY!" gasped King Thrum. "WHAT A TRICKSIE!"

"And to finish off," continued Lord Egbert, "I will also make MYSELF disappear!"

He lay down, pulled the napkin over his head with a flourish, and rolled through the crack, vanishing from sight.

Chapter 18

Underneath the table, Velda bounced off a giant's knee, swung down the table leg and landed on the ground. Sister Akuba somersaulted down behind her, and then came the others, one by one.

Lord Egbert was last, gliding down from the table on a wave of applause, his cape flapping behind him. "I do suggest we run!"

"Quick!" Velda led her crew on a sprint towards the doorway.

"OH, LOOKSIE!" came a giant's voice. "THE HOOMANS ARE ESCAPING!" King Thrum banged his fist on the table in excitement. "THEN WE WILL

HAVESIES A LIKKLE HOOMAN HUNT!"

Princess Gerda clapped her hands together. "YIPPEE! A HOOMAN HUNT! MY FAVOURITE GAMESIE!"

The giants got to their feet, which felt and sounded like an earthquake. Velda and her crew dashed out of the door.

"Come on!" Velda led them back towards the princess's room. Maybe there was some way to get up the belch stack? It wasn't much of a plan, but it was better than being dessert. And what about the hammer?

"Wait!" Bridie's eagle eye spotted some words carved high above an archway. "It says, The Library."

"SO?! We're a bit busy trying NOT TO BE EATEN right now!" cried Velda.

"But giants hate books. I dinnae know if you noticed, but they're not very smart. Why would they have something as useful as a library?"

"And look!" Sister Akuba pointed out some footprints in the dust leading under the archway. Velda remembered that the servant carrying the hammer had been barefoot. Maybe if they could find the hammer, they could have complete power over all the giants and avoid being munched!

"Right," Velda bellowed. "Change of plan, you lot! Follow me!"

"OORAH, Boss!" they cried, tracking the dusty footprints down some steep stone steps.

Behind them, the giants' voices were getting closer. "COME HERE, LIKKLE HOOMANSY-HOOMANS!"

Velda and her friends soon came to a massive door. There was no way through, but they spied a door handle halfway up.

"Leave it to me!" Sister Akuba vaulted off the ground, scaled the door, and then backflipped onto the handle and yanked it down.

As the door opened, it gave a mighty **CRREAAK!**

The giants heard it, their hulking figures appearing behind Velda and her crew. "OOH, HERE THEY ARESIES!" said Princess Gerda. "I'VE FOUNDS THE LIKKLE PUDDENS!"

"You get the hammer!" yelled Bridie to Velda. "I'll stay here and hold them off."

"How?" asked Velda.

"Och, how else!" Bridie twirled her griddle pan and gripped one of her frozen bannocks, before dropping it. "Oops!"

"I will help." Henna readied her bow. "And my friend, too." She launched her seagull into the air. "Poo, winged one! Poo like you have never pooed before!"

Velda and the others ran on, the sound of the bird's shrieking cry echoing behind them.

Chapter 19

Inside the Frost Giants' library, ice-blue torches lit GARGANTUAN bookcases, but they held only musty old cobwebs (and the odd human skeleton). It was the perfect hiding place for a treasure like the Frost Hammer – somewhere no other giant would bother to tread.

The footprints the crew were following led into the middle of the room, where there was a huge stone plinth. The velvet pillow the servant had been carrying sat on top, and perched on the pillow, was...

"The Frost Hammer!" cried Velda. She raced towards it.

Outside, Bridie batted her bannocks at the giants' feet and Henna fired her bow at their legs. Henna's seagull dive-bombed their enormous heads, splattering them with poo.

DOIN-NGGG!

THUP! THUP! THUP!

SPLAT!

But they were no match for the giants. "OUCHIE! OUCHIE!!" yelped King Thrum, but then he swooped down and scooped Bridie and Henna up in his hands, and plucked Henna's gull from the air. "GOTCHA! PESKY-WESKY HOOMANS!"

"THE REST OF THEMSIES ARE IN THERE!" shrieked Princess Gerda. They burst into the library, but instead of stopping Velda, they started arguing about who should get to scoff the hoomans (sorry, humans) first.

"REALLIES, IT SHOULD BE ME-SIES. I'M THE KING," declared Thrum.

Princess Gerda stuck out her bottom lip. "BUT IT'S MY WEDDEN DAY, DADDY-WADDY!"

"OH, ALRIGHTSIES!" said Thrum. "YOU WINSIES! BUT—"

Their arguments came to a crashing halt when Velda threw her grappling hook to the top of the plinth, climbed up and reached the hammer. "OI! You'll be eating no one today, giantsy-wiantsies!" She grasped the handle of the hammer. It was heavy in her hand, but with all her strength she hoisted it high into the air. The light from the torches illuminating the room caught the glittering frost of the hammer, sending shards of magical crystal-blue across the stone floor.

King Thrum gave a whimper. "OH DEARSIES!

I DO BELIEVE THAT SMALL HOOMAN HAS OUR FROST HAMMER!"

"That's right!" cried Velda. "And it's time you lot learned it's rude to try and eat your guests!"

With a huge **ROAR!**, she brought the hammer crashing down on the plinth with an almighty *SMASH!*

Chapter 20

Days later at Elsinore Castle, Count Stollenberg
was in his treasure room, his head in his hands. His
usually perfect hair resembled a birds' nest. His skin
was dull from lack of sleep. Though he'd stuck wax
in his ears, he still couldn't drown out the AWFUL
sound of Mandrake's singing. He'd wanted a bard,
NOT a torturer!

"PLEASE, I beg you, STOP! I've had enough, do
you understand? ENOUGH!" croaked Stollenberg.

Mandrake did indeed stop, but only so he could
break into another song.

TW-OINNNGGG!

"Enough, enough,
He says he's had enough..."

Stollenberg considered throwing Mandrake out of the window, but he figured it still wouldn't stop him singing. Then he considered throwing *himself* out of the window. He'd been counting the days since he'd sent that red-haired little girl off in search of the Frost Hammer. Where was she?!

A gigantic **CRASH!** interrupted Mandrake's next verse, as the treasure room door was smashed to smithereens. One of the count's guards staggered through, bruised and battered. Only half of his fancy feathered helmet was still perched on his head, as the top had been sliced clean off.

"I quit!" he whimpered, before collapsing face first to the floor.

A tiny figure climbed over him, whistling a jaunty tune. A mass of curly red hair poked out from under an oversized helmet.

"Velda!" Stollenberg stifled the urge to throw himself at her feet. "You're back!"

Mandrake strummed his harp.

TW-OINNNGGG!

"Ooorah! Ooraaah!
It is my boss, Veldaaaah!
It feels so fun, my friends have come—"

Velda threw her axe, which scythed through the air and sliced a cord that held up one of Stollenberg's tapestries. It tumbled off the wall, burying Mandrake under a mound of fabric.

"How do you do that?" gasped Stollenberg.

"Do what?" asked Velda.

"Get him to shut up. I've been trying for weeks!"

"Mandrake!" Velda called, and the bard poked his tufty head out. "Back to the ship. We're leaving."

Mandrake shrugged off the tapestry, then wiggled his fingers at Stollenberg. "Hoodle-too! I've enhoyed my jolliday!" And he skipped out.

"He said he enjoyed his holiday," said Velda with a smile.

"You're taking him back?! I mean, I'm glad and all, but... He's a weapon of mass destruction!" croaked Stollenberg.

"I know," said Velda, "and he's OUR weapon of mass destruction. Plus, I kinda missed him."

"You don't understand! I've got no guards left. Most of them quit because of his so-called 'singing'."

"Wimps!" Velda scoffed. "Anyway, about our deal." She whipped out the Frost Hammer, its magical blue light glimmering.

Stollenberg's icy eyes widened. "The Frost Hammer! You got it!"

"Yep. There's just one teensy change to our agreement." Velda casually strolled across the room, twirling the hammer.

"What do you mean?" the count demanded.

Velda winked, then smashed the hammer into the glowing white thorn bush standing in the corner.

Chapter 21

The thorn bush shattered to pieces like glass, its glow wisping away into the air.

"NOOOO!" Count Stollenberg howled. "What have you done?!"

"Soz, but I've broken your spell, Stollenberg," Velda said. "Or should I say, Prince Olaf. You see, I've figured it out – you're King Thrum's lost son. You ran away from home, taking that thorn tree with you, and used its magic to turn you into a human – and not a very nice one."

"Bu-Bu—" he spluttered. "Without it I'll turn back into a—"

Stollenberg was interrupted by the sound of his leather shoes ripping. His feet were growing, getting bigger and hairier by the second.

"I didn't buy your story," said Velda. "I mean, why go to all this trouble for a hammer? It didn't make any sense. Then I spotted the portraits of King Thrum's lost son with his piercing blue eyes, and saw the other white thorn bush in the giants' hall, and learned what the hammer could do – and I knew what was really going on. You wanted the hammer to protect your new life. To make sure no one could ever break your spell and force you to change back."

"You can't do this!" Stollenberg cried "It's not fair!" His hair started to turn snow white. "Giants are horrible and stupid and ugly, and, worst of all, they've got no idea about money, or style, or culture!"

"You ran away from home because you were different," said Velda kindly. "Because you didn't want to be who they expected you to be. I get that – so did I. But you're all alone here, and your family misses you."

"D-Do they really?" the count asked.

"Of course they do. Look, I can be a girl *and* a Viking, which means you can be a Frost Giant *and* a money-hungry twerp, or whatever else you want to be."

"I *am* so alone here." Stollenberg looked sad. "Do you think they'll really take me ba-ba-ba-BACKSIE?" His hands suddenly ballooned. "And accept me for who I AMSIES?"

"Oh, I think they might." Velda smiled, nodding at the window. The glass smashed to pieces and a TITANIC eyeball appeared.

"SON, IS THAT YOU-SIE?" boomed King Thrum's voice.

Stollenberg gave a cry. "DADDY-WADDYKINS?" Then his skin turned blue, his shoulders burst out of his expensive coat and his bottom exploded out of the seat of his trousers. Velda saw that it was time to make a sharp exit, and she leapt out of the window into King Thrum's palm.

From inside, she heard a wail, followed by a **BANG!**, a **CRASH!** and a **BOOM!** The castle walls shook and then a GARGANTUAN blue head burst through the roof, sending debris tumbling to the ground below. Another window smashed, and out shot Prince Olaf's huge hand. "HELP! I'M STUCKSIES!"

King Thrum laughed, a great thundering laugh like an avalanche. "MY BOY! DON'T WORRY, I WILL GET YOU OUTSIE!"

"OH DADDY-WADDYKINS, I AM SORRYWOZZLE!" blubbered Prince Olaf. He still had Stollenberg's icy blue eyes, but apart from that he was all Frost Giant.

King Thrum set Velda down on the ground, where she offered the Frost Hammer back to him. "Here you go. You'd better keep this."

"THAT IS VERY GOODSIE OF YOU, VELDA-WELDA," he replied, taking the hammer from her with pinched fingers.

"WHAT?" cried Prince Olaf. "YOU'RE JUST GOING TO GIVE IT BACKSIE? YOU COULD CONTROL ALL THE GIANTSES WITH THAT HAMMER!"

"Nah," said Velda with a shrug. "I've places to be, people to wallop, y'know." But before leaving them to it, she pointed a finger up at the king.

"Now remember, no eating humans!"

King Thrum nodded. "I WILL TRYSIES, VELDA-WELDA."

With that, Velda pushed a gobsmacked guard off his horse, hopped into the saddle and galloped off, leaving the castle and two hugging giants behind her.

Chapter 22

As Velda arrived at the harbour, she smiled to see her whole crew together again. She'd sent Sister Akuba and Henna to raid Stollenberg's private vault and swipe two sacks of silver for the nuns (plus the keys to their old convent), and two sacks for the crew, which was

the agreement. "Fair's fair," said Velda, patting the sacks as they were hoisted aboard.

"Fair's fair," agreed Henna. "And a reward for my friend." She nodded at her seagull companion, who was buried up to his beak in a barrel full of peanuts.

One of the old men on the harbourside ground his gums and shook his fist. "I knew you'd bring bad luck, you girl Vikings!"

Bridie tossed a rock-hard bannock into the air and whacked it with her iron griddle. *DO-INNGGG!*

It bounced off the old man's noggin, and he crumpled to the ground.

"Oops! Bad news. We're out of bannocks again," she said.

"Never fear, **The Great Egberto** is here!" Lord Egbert whisked off his top hat to reveal a single bannock balanced on top of his head.

"TA-DAAAAAH!"

"Wow, for once that was actually a braw trick," said Bridie.

"At last! I'm on a *roll*," announced the amateur magician, lifting the oaty breadcake off his head and flourishing it about. "*Roll*, get it?"

"Ugh, *dough* me a favour," laughed Sister Akuba.

"Stop *loafing* around, you villainous sea-weavils!" barked Velda with a smile.

"Sow about a hice nong?" asked Mandrake.

"A nice song?" Velda grinned. "Why not? Let rip, Mandrake!"

TW-OINNNGGG!

But before the bard could burst into song, Velda interrupted him with a cry: "That's quite enough of that! Now get rowing you snivelling pig-dogs!"

The crew rowed the *Mangy Mutt* through the harbour entrance and out into the open sea, hoisting the sail with a cry of "OORAH, BOSS! OORAH!"

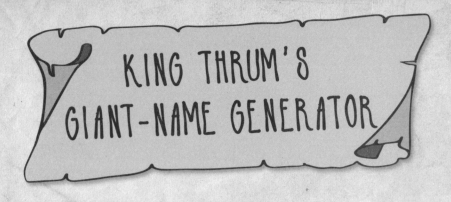

KING THRUM'S GIANT-NAME GENERATOR

King Thrum is delighted to be giving out giant names to his favourite hoomans (before he eats them for dessert, of course!). Find out yours below…

1. What's the *first* letter of your *first* name? Your giant first name begins with the same letter.

A. Achy	**J.** Jolly	**S.** Splatsie
B. Burpsy	**K.** Kindsy	**T.** Twitsy
C. Cutesy	**L.** Loudsy	**U.** Upsie
D. Dipsy	**M.** Meansy	**V.** Vomitsy
E. Eggsy	**N.** Nosey	**W.** Whoopsie
F. Fartsy	**O.** Oopsie	**X.** Xcellentsy*
G. Grumpsy	**P.** Poopsie	**Y.** Yawnsy
H. Hairy	**Q.** Quacksy	**Z.** Zippy
I. Itchy	**R.** Rudesy	

*Please note: Giants are *really* bad at spelling.

2. In which *month* were you born? Use that to find your giant surname.

Jan: Enormous   **Jul:** Jumbo
Feb: Gigantical   **Aug:** Gargantuan
Mar: Humungous   **Sept:** Monster-mega
Apr: Immense   **Oct:** Colossal
May: Mahoosive   **Nov:** Stupendous
Jun: Ginormous   **Dec:** Whopper-doodle-do

3. Which fun activity would you rather do? This will tell you what *kind* of giant you are.

a) Skiing = you're a **Frost Giant**
b) Scuba-diving = you're a **Sea Giant**
c) Building a treehouse = you're a **Forest Giant**
d) Toasting marshmallows over a campfire =
       you're a **Fire Giant**

Put all of your answers together and TA-DAA!
Nowsies you have your giant name!

For Example

David MacPhail was born in May and his fun activity
would be skiing, so his giant name is

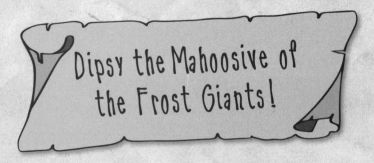

Dipsy the Mahoosive of
the Frost Giants!

What would your giant name be? What about your
friends' and family members' giant names?

My name is _____ the _____

of the _____

Thorfinn the Nicest Viking
Chief's House
Indgar Village
NORWAY

Velda the Awesomest Viking
The Mangy Mutt
THE SEA

Dearest Velda,

I hope you are having the most wonderful time on your adventures! All is well here in Indgar Village, thankfully no sign of another **Awful Invasion**, though Dad has been talking about hosting the **Gruesome Games** next year.

Remember the **Rotten Scots** who kidnapped me that one time? They came to visit recently, they said hi!

I've been perfecting a new recipe for scones and Gertrude the Grotty says they're much better than anything from the **Disgusting Feast**.

I thought I saw a party of **Raging Raiders** in the bay last week, but turns out they were just advertising a new spa retreat. Mum is going to check it out.

The Mangy Elks Protection League are making good use of the **Terrible Treasure**: they've treated the Elks to their favourite dinner, mashed turnips.

Have you seen the **Dreadful Dragon** on your travels? The whole country is still talking about that epic battle with the dragonslayer! Except Oswald, who has been very busy with some **Putrid Potions**...

Please write to tell me when you're next passing, we all miss you terribly!

With love and best wishes,

Thorfinn x x x

P.S. Please feed Percy the Pigeon once he's delivered this letter!

P.P.S. I've been trying awfully hard to follow your advice and act like a proper Viking, but the world is just too lovely to be angry. I hope you understand!

RICHARD THE PICTURE-CONQUEROR

DAVID THE STORY-CHIEF

DAVID MACPHAIL has worked as a chicken wrangler, a ghost-tour guide and a waiter on a tropical island, and now has the sensible job of writing about yetis and Vikings. At home in Perthshire, Scotland, he exists on a diet of cream buns and zombie movies.

RICHARD MORGAN was born and raised by goblins on the Yorkshire moors. After running away to New Zealand to play with yachts and paint backgrounds for Disney TV he returned to the UK to write and illustrate children's books. He now lives in Cambridge, England, and has a family of goblins of his own.

David and Richard are the creators of the *Velda the Awesomest Viking* and *Thorfinn the Nicest Viking* series.